AF491086

Short & Sweet Interracial Romance: Bundle # 1

Short & Sweet Interracial Romance, Volume 1

Remy Marie

Published by Remy Marie, 2023.

This is a work of fiction. Similarities to real people, places, or events are entirely coincidental.

SHORT & SWEET INTERRACIAL ROMANCE: BUNDLE # 1

First edition. August 16, 2023.

Copyright © 2023 Remy Marie.

ISBN: 979-8223300441

Written by Remy Marie.

Table of Contents

Finding True Love
Chapter 1

"Do you think I'll ever find love?" I asked my best friend, Heather. She shrugged.

"I don't know why you're rushing it. This is your prime of your life, Gina. I mean, you're only twenty-five. You should be living up your twenties. Find love in your thirties."

"I'm tired of all that," Heather. "I want love now. I'm tired of all the games and the clubs. Why can't I just have a deep connection with someone? That's why I signed up for an online dating website."

Heather laughed and shook her head. "I'm telling you it's a mistake. Don't rush this. Just let it flow."

"I can't. I'm lonely. This life of being single isn't for me. Please just support me on this."

Heather sighed and shrugged. "Fine. I got you, but these relationships built online aren't real. Hell, how do you know if this guy is even real?"

"Isn't that the point of love? Taking a chance at love?"

"It's a wild shot in the dark though..."

"But if I'm right, it could be the romance I'm looking for."

"True. What site are you on?"

"True Love Singles.com."

"Ah the one where a matchmaker puts you together with someone? Have you matched with anyone yet?"

"There were some."

"Oh, let me see." Heather took my phone from me and looked through my matches. "What about him. He's cute."

I bit my lip and rubbed my elbow. "He's black."

"So? You said it yourself, you're looking for a real connection. The system seems to believe that you two are compatible."

"I know but he's a black guy. I'm not racist or anything but…"

Heather laughed. "But what? What's there to question? You wanted a guy. He's a guy."

"I know but…"

"You see this is why I wanted you to wait til thirty. You're not ready. If you were ready something like race wouldn't matter. Everyone knows that true love is built off our connections. If your afraid to build one because of race, then what's the point?"

I didn't know how to answer her as I stared back at her.

She laughed and shook her head. "Figures. I'm heading out, but you need to decide. Are you looking for love or not? If you are, text the guy." Heather waved goodbye and left my apartment.

Chapter 2

Later that night I stared at the picture of the black man I was matched with. His name was Kyle. He had a great smile and an athletic frame. However, there was something telling me I shouldn't message him. I know it's cliché to say that I'm not racist, but if I had to choose, I would rather be with a white guy. However, Kyle checked a lot of my boxes. I sighed and realized that Heather was right. If I wanted to find love, I had to take a chance.

I clicked on his profile and messaged him.

Me: Hi, we matched online. How are you?

I rolled my eyes the moment I sent the message.

God what am I doing, I wondered.

A few minutes later I got a message back.

Kyle: Hi, Gina. I'm happy you reached out to me. I'm doing good. Just got off a long day of work. I'm ready for the weekend. How are you doing?

Me: Good. This is actually my first time reaching out to someone on here. It's all new to me.

Kyle: Me too. You're not alone.

Kyle then sent me a gif of Michael Jackson singing, *You Are Not Alone*. I laughed and shook my head.

Me: That's funny.

Kyle: I thought it would be. Honestly I joined this site because I'm looking for a deep connection. I'm looking for love.

Me: Yeah that's me too.

Kyle: What's your reason for love?

Me: I want to find someone to spend the rest of my life with. I'm tired of the games. What about you?

Kyle: I want a family.

Me: That's sweet. So do I.

Kyle: Yeah, I know it's cliché but I want the whole two kids, house in the suburbs and a dog or two. I want it all. So far I have the good paying job, I just need the right woman to marry.

Me: What's your job?

Kyle: Oh, I'm a CPA.

Me: That's pretty vanilla.

Kyle: I'm a pretty vanilla guy, which happens to be my favorite ice cream flavor.

I laughed as my smile grew larger.

Me: I like chocolate.

Kyle: perhaps we should go on an ice cream date? Take a stroll around the park. We can keep talking like this. I like talking to you, Gina.

I grinned and closed my eyes. I didn't know what to say. Honestly, a part of me was afraid to see what would happen if this relationship grew while the other part of me knew that Kyle could be the guy I was looking for.

It was one date, what was the worst that could happen, I questioned.

I took a deep breath and texted him back.

Me: Sure. What park?

Kyle: Meet me at Sunset Park, at 6 pm. Bailey's Ice Cream. Do you know where that's at?"

Me: Yeah, I do. I'll see you there.

I bit my lip, and my heart was pounding. I had a date. The only question now was what was I going to wear.

Chapter 3

I spent most of the day trying to decide what I should wear. Ultimately, I decided to wear a white sun dress and a pair of gladiator sandals. I wore my brunette hair down and had silver hoop earrings and a golden bracelet around my wrist. When I arrived at the ice cream parlor I got out of my car and headed towards the front.

Based on Kyle's picture I spotted him. He was taller than I expected. His skin was dark, and he had a small afro. Like me he wore jeans, had on a white polo shirt and a pair of shades rested on his forehead. The moment he saw me his smile triple in size.

"Gina!" He waved.

"Hi..." I gave him a small smile. His eyes lingered on me, and he made my heart leap. The way he looked at me was different. It wasn't like he was undressing me with his eyes. It was more like I took his breath away. His eyes got wider the longer he stared.

"Gina, you look amazing."

"Thanks," I grinned pushing back a strand of my hair behind my ear. His line was simple, but it was doing it for me. Enough to make me blush.

"You look great too." I replied.

He grinned at me and then nodded towards the ice cream parlor. Shall we?"

"Yes, thank you. This is actually a first for me. Usually, my first date we go to a restaurant. I like this."

"Yeah, I'm over the whole steak dinner thing. Let's be rebels."

"Ha, rebel scum. I like it."

"Rebel Scum? Wait, are you a Star Wars fan?"

"Huge. I know it's not super girly, but my dad was a huge Star Wars fan. We watched all of the movies."

"Your dad sounds like a great guy."

"He was a great guy..." my voice trailed off.

"Oh, Gina...I'm so sorry."

"It's okay. He died three years ago. It's just been my mom and I since."

"Oh, I'm sorry. I can't imagine losing my parents."

"It's okay. Thank you though." I grinned. We got into the line for ice cream and Kyle asked, "so did you want your chocolate ice cream in a cone or cup."

"Waffle cone. Are you crazy?"

He laughed. "Nope, once more I like the way you think Gina."

We walked up to the counter and Kyle ordered two ice cream cones. Once we got our dessert, we walked the lake and kept talking. I loved talking to Kyle. Talking with him was so natural and easy. The way our comments went from one thing to the other. I was beginning to see why the matchmakers put us together. We had so much in common between likes in music and shows, including ideals and beliefs. Most importantly he made me laugh. I felt lighter than air every time I laughed.

The date was going so good that neither of us wanted to go home. So instead of ending the date after getting ice cream we decided to walk to a nearby fast-food restaurant to eat hamburgers. After ordering two burgers and fries we took our food to the lake and sat on a bench nearby.

"Here's your burger," Kyle said, handing me the sandwich.

"Thank you.," I opened the wrapper, took a bite, and groaned from the charred beef taste

"Is it good?" He chuckled.

"You have no idea." I laughed, taking another bite.

He grinned and took a bite of his fry before chowing down on the burger.

"I'm really liking this date so far."

"Me too," I grinned.

"Is it safe to assume, we're going on another one?"

"Presumptuous much?" I laughed.

"Hey, I'm bold. That's why you like me."

I laughed. "It's one of your finer qualities. Yeah, I wouldn't mind a date with you. This was fun."

"Good." Kyle smirked. He stared at me again but this time it gave me shivers. The way he looked at me felt like he was looking into my soul. *What was wrong with me*, I wondered.

I felt like I was under his spell. With every second, I felt myself growing closer and closer to him. I never would've thought I would feel this way about someone I met on the internet, but Kyle was a whole lot more than what I expected.

"Oh, you have something on your lip. Looks like ketchup. May I?" He asked with a napkin in his hand.

I nodded and he blotted the crevice of my mouth. His brown eyes stared into mine as he cleaned me. His fingers grazed my skin and I shivered. I didn't know what was coming over me. My insides felt like they were on fire. My desire burned for him like never before. I knew this was our first date, but there was something about Kyle that made me want to scream.

After our burger, we walked hand and hand in the park. We walked until the moon shined on the lake. For that time, we spent together it felt like time stood still. I didn't want the night to end. I didn't want to stop talking and laughing with Kyle. It was like I was swept up in my emotions with him. He was such a sweet gentleman, and I was wrong thinking about what I said initially. I felt like such a fool to judge him by his race.

"Kyle?"

"Yeah?"

"I just wanted to let you know that this date was more than I expected. I wanted to be truthful to you and I hope it doesn't change your opinion of me, but I don't want to keep anything from you."

"Okay...you can tell me anything."

I took a deep breath and then looked him in his eyes. "Although the matchmakers put us together, I was hesitant to go on this date because I've never dated a black man. I was scared because I didn't know what to expect. I know we live in the 21st century and everything, but interracial couples still have a stigma in this country and..."

"Gina, it's okay. I was a bit hesitant too."

"Really?"

He nodded. "When I was matched with you, I was shocked. I mean, I've mostly dated black women, but I was being serious when I told you I was looking for a life partner. I don't care what your skin color is, or if your short or tall. I don't care about any of your physical features. All I care about is if you're a good person and if I could see the rest of my life with you."

"And where do you see us?"

"I can see us growing old together, walking the park just like we're doing now."

"Oh, Kyle, that's sweet." I grinned.

"You're worth it, Gina. You're worth every penny." His eyes lingered on mine again. My body caught a stray chill and I trembled. I sensed he was inching closer to me, and I did the same. The tension between us was high and I felt this magnetic energy pulling me towards him.

"Gina?"

"Yes..." I mumbled.

"May I seal this amazing first date with a kiss?"

"Yes," I breathed.

Before I could register what was happening, I felt his lips on mine. His hand rested on the small of my back as he tilted me. My legs felt like jello and my head felt light. The feeling of his lips on top of mine was nothing like I expected. He tasted like mint which surprised me. The longer we kissed the more I wanted him as my arms wrapped around his body. My heart felt like it was on fire. It was filled with desire and lust as my grip on him tighten.

When he finally let me go, I felt like screaming and begging for more. It took a few seconds for me to compose myself as I breathed deeply several times.

"Wow that was..."

"Amazing?"

I nodded. "Nothing like what I expected."

"Would it be bad to ask for a second?"

I laughed and shook my head, "I would be offended if you didn't."

He laughed and lifted me up. He spun me around, placed me on my feet, and rocked my world yet again with a wonderful kiss.

Chapter 4

Kyle and I've been dating for two wonderful months. Every day with him was amazing. Every date we went on I looked forward for the next one. My feelings for Kyle were like no other. I never dated a man like him. He made me smile from every phone call, text and meet up. Not to mention the physical sexuality he presented to me. Where I once doubted, I could be physically attracted to a black man, those thoughts had morphed into lust as I craved for that first night we could become intimate.

Even though we officially became girlfriend and boyfriend, we were both taking it slow in the sex department. It's not to say that we were complete prudes. Things still got steamy in the bedroom, but we were saving sex for our our second month dating anniversary, which was today.

I honestly had no idea what he planned for us. All I knew was I had to be up early, had to dress for a hot climate, and we were going to be gone for the weekend.

Kyle showed up at my door, and grinned. "Wow Gina you look amazing. I love those short shorts on you." He admired my outfit that included shorts, and a green tank top.

"Thank you, you look sexy too..." I grinned, looking at his jean shorts and polo shirt.

"Are you ready to go?"

I nodded. "Can you finally tell me where we're going?"

He laughed. "I guess the cat is out of the bag now. You'd figure it out sooner or later when we got to the airport. We're flying to Orlando for the day to go to Disney World and their Star Wars Galaxy's Edge!"

"What!" I screamed. I'm pretty sure I woke up all of my neighbors, but I didn't care. Going to Galaxy Edge was all I wanted to do since the park opened. I've dreamed about this and the fact that Kyle was making it a reality put me on cloud 9. I jumped into his arms and kissed him.

"Kyle! How? I mean park tickets are expensive, not to mention the airfare and hotel stay..."

"For you, it's worth every penny."

I grinned and kissed him once more. "How did I luck out with such a great man?"

"It wasn't luck. It was fate..." he muttered before kissing me again. He took my breath away with that passionate kiss. He placed his forehead on mine and caressed my cheek. "We need to get going if we're going to make this flight."

"Can't we stay here and make out?"

"Damn, girl, I would love to, let's save that for tonight."

"Perfect." I grinned.

He kissed me once more and picked up my overnight bag by the door.

"Shall we?" I nodded and took his hand exiting my apartment.

We drove to the airport and took a flight to Orlando. By the time we landed it was only 10 am in the morning. We dropped our bags off at the hotel and then went straight to the park. We had the best time there. We laughed with glee, took pictures, we built our lightsabers, and experienced the ultimate Star Wars experience. We stayed until the park closed and took a ride back to our hotel nearby.

Walking into our room, Kyle closed the door behind him and placed his arms around me. "Did you have a good time?"

"I did. What a two-month anniversary. I can't wait to see what you do to top our three months."

"Umm Disneyland?"

"Of course. What was I thinking?"

He laughed and kissed me. He held me tightly and looked into my eyes making me shiver.

"Gina?"

"Yeah?"

"I never felt this way about a woman before. Every day I'm with you feels like a gift. Do you remember what we talked about on our first date? About finding true love?"

"Yes, you said when you found it you never wanted to let it go."

"Yes, I feel that way now. Call me crazy. I know we've only been together for two months, but in those two months I've fallen for the most beautiful woman in the world. Every day with you makes me smile. I crave these moments right here. These small loving tender moments. I want to have these for the rest of my life. That is why I love you."

The moment I heard him say the words, I love you, my eyes got wider. I stared into his brown eyes, and I felt a strong emotion in my heart. Right there I realized I felt the same. I didn't hesitate as I told him, "I love you too."

He grinned and kissed me once more. As we kissed, I felt his tongue enter my mouth and I moaned as he massaged mine. My hands wrapped around his body and held him tightly. He ground his body on mine and I could feel his stiffness.

"I want you..." I uttered.

"I want you too..." he groaned. I felt his hands lower to my shorts. He pushed them away and then pushed my panties to the side. I felt his finger enter me and I moaned.

"Oh, Kyle..." His finger jagged in and out of me making me twist and turn. I felt like a puppet as he moved me at his will. I placed my head on his neck and sucked on his skin. He groaned and I felt his finger wiggle quicker between my thighs.

My hands drifted down to his belt, and I unbuckled him, and unbuttoned his pants. My hand drifter lower to his boxers, where my hand slipped in, and I stroked him. He groaned once more and closed his eyes. I could tell my actions were having the desired effect.

"On the bed..." he commanded. There was this certain huskiness in his voice that made my legs weak. As I walked toward the bed, I could hear Kyle remove his clothes, so I did the same. By the time I laid on the bed, we were both naked.

I turned to see a fully naked Kyle and I swear my heart stopped. Damn did he look good. His muscular figure had six pack and as my eyes drifter lower I saw his manhood. He was long, thick and hard. My insides trembled as I knew that in a few moments he would be inside me.

He laid on the bed in front of me and spread my legs. He was in complete control as my thighs quivered. He leaned forward and licked my folds. The moment I felt his tongue in me I was heaven. I gripped the sheets like they were a lifeline as my my pleasure increased exponentially.

"Oh Kyle." I moaned. My fingers combed through his afro as he brought me pleasure that I never felt before. His fingers and tongue explored parts of my body I didn't even know were there. He spun my world around and opened my mind to new possibilities. Ever touch, every flick, and every lick brought me pleasure like no other. My body was trembling, and I felt like I was going to pop. I closed my eyes and yelled as I came. My whole body shook when I experienced my powerful orgasm.

"Kyle, that was amazing," I breathed.

"You taste good, but I want the real thing."

"You want me to help you?"

He shook his head. "I've been waiting for this moment for a while now. I've been ready. Hold on, let me get a condom." He walked to his bag and took out a foil wrapper. He rolled the white rubber over his cock and then walked over.

He laid in bed and kissed me. He stared into my eyes and held my cheek.

"I love you."

"I love you too," I repeated.

He grinned and then entered me. I groaned the moment I felt him inside. He felt amazing. It was a perfect fit. Just feeling him stretch me out was the greatest feeling. He was like no other man I ever had before. The way he touched me. The way he kissed me. The way he fucked me. There was something about the way he made love to me that I swooned for.

He was aggressive yet passionate. He was loving yet dominating. He was everything I wanted in a man.

He held my legs back and buried his cock in me. He was machine as he kept pumping in and out of me. I held his back as I was taken to that special place once more. I closed my eyes and came once more. He wasn't far behind as he groaned. I felt him finish in his condom and he pulled out of me. He tossed the condom to the side and held me.

"Kyle, that was amazing."

"It sure was. Goddamn, do I love you."

"I love you too," I grinned. I leaned forward and kissed him. Our lips stayed locked until he pulled away. He rubbed my cheek and stared into my eyes.

"Gina, I know it's only been two months, but I know what we have is special. I can't see myself with no other woman than you."

"Me too."

"Can I ask you a question?"

"Sure..."

"One second." He got out bed and walked towards his bag and pulled out a small box. I recognized it immediately and my heart started to race.

"Kyle..."

"Gina, I want you to know that I plan on treating you right for the rest of your life. When we both met, we talked about finding love. I've found my love and I don't plan on letting it go. Gina, will you marry me?" He opened the box and I saw a diamond ring inside. I shrieked and kissed him.

He laughed, "Is that a yes?"

"Of course! Yes, I will marry you!"

He grinned and kissed me once more. "I love you, Gina."

"And I love you too, Kyle."

I kissed him once more sealing our love forever.

Looking back at it, I find it funny my initial hesitations about being with Kyle, but they were overblown. Kyle was perfect for me. He was my true love. After that night, our love had grown, and we both got the happy ending we wanted. We had two kids, had a house in the suburbs and two dogs. Our love was everlasting and prefect. Who would've thought I found all of this online?

My True Love
Chapter 1

Standing in front of the bathroom mirror, I combed my red hair with my fingers, trying to get the best look. It had been a month since my boyfriend and I had slept together and tonight I planned on changing our dry spell. I had placed on some sexy lingerie that filled out my curves and was ready to surprise him with an impromptu strip tease.

I had been taking some lessons on how to give a seductive lap dance, and was ready to show them to my boyfriend, Keith.

God do I hope this will get us out of our funk.

For the last couple of months, Keith had been distant. No matter what I did he always was on his phone or not wanting to be near or talk to me. In the beginning Keith and I were great, so much so that I moved into his apartment and we'd been together for years, now it just seemed like we were on autopilot.

I'm not sure why either. We were a good fit for each other, well I at least thought that.

Taking one last look in the mirror, I grinned and walked out of the ensuite bathroom into the bedroom, where Keith was watching the baseball game, and texting.

Not once did he look up.

Attempting to get his attention, I cleared my voice.

"Yeah, one second, Rita." Keith mumbled not looking up from his phone.

"Babe...look..."

"I said one second." He snapped back as if I was distracting him. I narrowed my brow and stomped in front of him.

"You got to be kidding me. Keith, look up. Look what I'm wearing."

Keith paused a second and glanced at my outfit.

"Looks nice, Rita. Just let me finish his email."

I rolled my eyes. He was always writing emails.

"Keith...baby, the email can wait. I can't. I'm so horny."

"Rita... seriously. I can't." Keith stood and attempted to walk out the room.

"Keith? What the fuck?" I beat him to the doorway and stood in front of him. " I'm half naked, ready to fuck and your first reaction is to get up and walk away."

"I told you. I'm busy."

I sighed and looked at his phone. Surprisingly, I see a text message pop on his screen.

"Busy? Who are you texting?"

"No, one."

"Bullshit. You're not writing an email. I can tell. Give me your phone. Now."

"No, it's mine. Whom I text is my business."

My heart beat increased as I suddenly had a suspicion that Keith was unfaithful. I glared at Keith with my hand out.

"Keith, give me the damn phone. Now!"

Keith yelled at me and shook his head. "No."

"Are you serious Keith? Just give me the fucking phone."

"Whom I text is my business."

Holding back the tears, I questioned, "Is it another woman?"

"No..."

"Keith please. Don't play dumb. If you're going to fuck someone behind my back, be a man about it. Own it."

Keith hesitated and closed his eyes. "Yes, I'm with someone."

"Why?"

Keith paused. "I don't love you anymore. Over the last months we've grown apart. Not to mention, you've stopped taking care of yourself. Gaining weight and..."

"What does gaining weight have to do with it?"

"Don't twist my words. Don't make me to be the asshole."

"No, you're doing that yourself. Calling me fat?"

"I didn't say that."

"You might as well had. Seriously, Keith, why are you just now saying this? When were you going to tell me?"

"I was waiting on the opportune time."

Tears began to flow down my face and I shook my head.

"Keith…"

"I'm sorry, Rita, but it's over for us. I think you should go."

"Go? Keith it's the middle of the night. Where am I going to go?"

"I don't care, but this between us is done. Go."

"No, I let's talk about this."

"There's nothing to talk about Rita. You and me, are done. That's it. Get dressed and leave. You can get the rest of your shit tomorrow."

I wanted to say more, but I couldn't. Tears rolled down my cheeks as I stomped away. I'd never been more embarrassed in my life. I quickly placed in a pair of sweats and a t-shirt, and found some sandals near the door. Keith followed me around the apartment, silently judging me. After getting my car keys, phone and wallet, I look at Keith one last time.

"Keith, please, let's just talk this out."

"I'm done with talking. Go." He unlocked the door and pushed me out.

Standing in the doorway, I watched as the door was slammed in front of me. I slumped my shoulders and cried as I'd never been more embarrassed in my life. Keith and I loved each other, or at least I thought he did. We were supposed to be together forever, but all of that turned out to be a lie.

Chapter 2

Driving down the street, I called my best friend of fourteen years, Bryson.

"Rita? It's one am." He groaned.

"Bryson. I need a place to stay." I cried.

I could hear the alertness in his voice when he growled, "what happened?"

"Keith and I...we broke up. He kicked me out..."

"You can come over."

"Thanks, Bryson."

I drove across town to Bryson's three bedroom house. Unlike Keith, Bryson owned his own home. It was a small ranch home with three bedrooms and one bathroom. Bryson was single, with no roommates so he used one room as an office/ guest room and the other as a gaming geek space. I called Bryson because I knew he had no one else staying with him.

When I arrived, Bryson was standing outside. His eyes were narrowed as I drove my beat up Nissan Maxima up his driveway.

Byron was a tall and lanky black man. If he had any athletic ability he'd be the starter on a basketball team, but Bryson's talents laid elsewhere, like computers and finance, which is why he was an accountant at a local CPA firm.

He was wearing a pair of black shorts and a Star Wars shirt, with some slides, when he walked down the steps to greet me.

Opening the car door, I smiled at him.

"Thanks for taking me in, Bryson."

He studied my face, before giving me a hug.

"Are you okay? He didn't hit you or anything?"

"No, I'm good. We just got into a huge fight. I have to move out tomorrow."

"Why tomorrow?"

"He's cheating on me. I guess he wants to get me out of his place so he can start seeing whomever on the reg."

"That fucker."

"Damn right."

"I just need a place to crash tonight, then I guess I'll move in with my parents tomorrow."

Bryson shook his head. "No, you can stay with me."

"You serious?"

"Ya, Rita. You've been my best friend since the 8th grade. I got your back no matter what."

I grinned. "Thanks, Bryson."

Bryson nodded and led me inside his house. The front door led to the living room, which contained a sofa, two chairs and a large flatscreen.

Bryson stood in the center and asked, "Did you want to stay up and talk about it?"

"Oh, I don't want to keep you."

"Rita, I always have time for you. Sit." He sat on the black couch and I sat next to him, placing my head on his shoulder. He held me close as I sobbed in his shoulder.

"Tonight was just a normal night. I actually planned on sleeping with him tonight. You know it's been a while for us."

"Yeah, I know."

"So, I get in some sexy underwear to surprise him and when I walk out he's texting."

Bryson nodded, following along.

"So I confront him and he gets defensive not letting me see his phone. That's when I see the text message. I question him about that and he finally admits that he's cheating on me."

"Damn."

"Yeah, I ask why and he says we drifted apart, and I've let myself go, getting fat."

Bryson shook his head. "Fat? You're beautiful."

I blushed and looked away. "You're too kind, Bryson."

He turned my head towards him. He peered into my eyes, making my body shiver.

"No, seriously. You are. Keith was a damn fool. I'd never liked him."

"Really? Why did you not say anything?"

"You liked him. I had my doubts, but I trusted your judgment."

I laughed. "Well, next time speak up. You could've saved me three years."

He chuckled. "Sorry. So what now?"

"I guess I'm back on the dating pool. Ugh, just saying it gives me the chills. What's it like out there?"

"Oh, it's bad. It's a dog eat dog type of experience. You'd be fine, though. A girl like you won't last on the market for long."

I laughed. "Thanks. Once again you're too good for me." I patted his leg and stood up. I walked around his living room, looking at the various pictures he had up. Most of them were his family. There was some of our friends from middle school and high school. I spotted our prom picture and grinned.

"Prom was so much fun that year wasn't it?"

"Depends on who your asking. You had a date with Tommy Bunch, while I went stag."

"Hey, I saw you dancing with Kelly Deer."

"Yeah, but Kelly wasn't the one who I wanted to dance with."

I rolled my eyes. "Hey now, Tommy already asked me by the time you worked up the courage to say something."

"You're never going to let me live that down are you?"

I shrugged and continued to look at the various pictures of Bryson and me through the years. I stopped at recent picture of Keith and me and turned away.

"Do you ever wonder what if?"

"What do you mean?" He asked.

"I mean, what if you asked me to prom instead of Tommy. If I would have said yes to you, I never had went with Tommy, and then would had dated Tommy and met Keith, whom I dated next, wasting three years of my life with. If I would have went with you, I would have avoid all of this pain I'm feeling."

"Why me?"

"You're a good guy, Bryson. Not many men are waking up at one am in the morning to talk to me. You're a good friend."

Bryson nodded. "Is that all you think of me?"

"What do you mean?"

"Just a friend. I've always been that. What happens if I wanted more?"

"More?" I shivered at the word.

Bryson stood up and stared into my eyes. His lingering stare took my breath away making it hard to breathe.

"You and I have been playing this cat and mouse game since grade school. Back in high school I was too afraid to tell you how I feel. Now I am. I'm ready. Do you believe in fate?"

"Bryson what are you saying." I knew it in my heart, but I had to hear the words.

"I'm in love you with, Rita. I've always have been. For years, I thought I was a fool for waiting for you. I thought I was crazy that I waited for you, but here you are, in my home, single. Is it fate, I don't know, but I do know I'm not letting you walk out that door, without knowing I love you."

"This is crazy Bryson. Soulmates? It's a bit too far."

"Is it. Admit it, there's been an attraction between us." He stood next to me. Our faces were a mere inch apart. With two fingers he tilted my chin up. Our eyes connected as we stared at each other.

"Admit it, you feel this invisible force pulling us together."

"Bryson..." I whispered. I couldn't find the words. There was something that was pulling me towards him. Perhaps it was the emotion of the night, or perhaps it was something else. A lingering connection that I too wanted to explore.

"Admit it. You want me, just as much as I want you."

"Bryson, I just broke up with Keith..."

"I know this is sudden, but I also know that you are the most beautiful woman in my life. I love every inch of you. Every curve, every shape, every wrinkle. You're my queen that I would bow to for the rest of my life. I was a fool for letting you go before. I don't plan on doing that again. I see an opening and I want to take what's mine, because this time I don't plan on letting go. Those fools you dated weren't for you, but I am. I am yours. Which is why I'm letting you decide. Say yes, and we see where this goes. Say no, and I'll say good night and go to my room."

My lips trembled at his powerful words. I'd never had a man fight for me like Bryson did. His eyes spoke the truth and I knew Bryson long enough to know that when he plants his flag, he doesn't retreat. I was scared of the future, but at the moment all I wanted to do was live in the present.

"Yes." I whispered.

Bryson smiled and leaned closer to my lips, I closed the gap placing my lips on his. I groaned feeling his soft touch. I felt his hands explore my body. The heat in my core grew as a want ached in my heart. He held me tightly, deepening his kiss. He bend me back, taking full advantage of me.

I felt his tongue slip in my mouth. He tasted like peppermint. His aroma drove me insane. The thoughts of Keith drifted from my brain as it became only Bryson and me.

"May I?" He asked, holding on to the hem of my sweatpants.

I nodded.

"No, I need you to say it. Tell me you want me."

"I want you. Bryson. I want you to feel you inside me. I need it. Please make love to me." I breathed.

"As you wish, my love."

His deep voice made me tremble. I didn't know what the night would bring, but I wasn't going to protest.

He kissed me once more as his hands slipped my sweats down to my ankles, and a second later I felt my shirt lifted up.

"Goddamn," I heard him mutter looking at my lingerie.

"Now I know he's a fool. He should be locked up for letting you leave the house like that."

"You like that?" I asked, modeling the outfit for him.

He nodded.

"Good, I had a dance for him. Care if I show it off for you?"

"I'd love it."

"Sit down."

He sat on the couch, legs sprawled out. I did my routine slowly and seductively. My eyes never broke contact with him as I twerked in front of him.

"Goddamn," he muttered. His eyes got wide as if my curves were hypnotizing him. I danced closer to him and straddled his waist. I slowly ground my hips over his crotch and felt his erection grow. His hands gripped my waist. He held me tightly as I twisted my body over his.

"This is some routine," he groaned.

"You like it?"

"I fucking love it." He growled. His hands slid down my shoulders to my breasts. He squeezed them and pushed them together.

"Keith was a loser to let you go. Your body should have been worshipped by him, not despised. I could drink you up."

His hands left my breasts and inched towards my crotch. His fingers slipped past my thong and inside my wet center. I moaned, feeling him circling around.

"Damn, you're so wet."

"What are you waiting for?" I found myself asking.

He grinned and rolled me over to my back. Laying on the couch, I watched as he took off my panties. I breathed deeply watching him inched towards my wet center. As soon as I felt his tongue, I moaned. Feeling him lick and touch every crevice, I was in heaven. My back arched as I was transported away from my troubles. My skin felt like it was on fire, and I gasped for air. I watched, Bryson's head bob as his tongue inched deeper in my folds. I was a sloppy mess, moaning like a banshee, but who could blame me, it felt so fucking good. It had been a while since a man pleasured me and I enjoyed every second of it.

I came hard. Really hard. So hard that I thought I was having a heart attack, but I didn't care. The sex was good. Really good.

I closed my eyes and gasped for air. My lungs burned from the exhaustion.

"Fuck, Bryson..." I muttered.

He looked up, wiped his face, and grinned at me. He didn't need to say anything. He could see on my face that he did his job.

"I'll be right back."

"Where are you going?" I asked. My voice was filled with need as I watched him disappear into the hallway. He returned naked, wearing a condom on his hard cock. My eyes didn't stray from his erect member. He sat back on the couch and laid on top of me.

"Are you ready?" He asked.

I nodded.

"No. I need you to say it again. Tell me that you want me."

"I want you. I was a fool before, but now I see that you're the man for me. Bryson please make love to me."

He grinned and kissed me passionately once more. As our lips stayed connected, I felt him slip inside. Slowly, he pumped in and out of me.

He kissed my neck and nuzzled his head there. Softly, I heard him whisper my name. The way he said it was full of emotion. It nearly brought me to tears. He truly wanted me. He wanted this to happen. There was something magical about having him. Laying there, I never felt more connected. I held the back of his head, begging him for more.

We were both taken by each other. He held me tightly thrusting slowly, and my hands slipped to the back of his ass, enjoying the pulsating pleasure that came.

He gradually increased his speed. As he did, we both became louder. The couch shifted from his powerful thrusts. He growled, as if he was a man possessed.

"Rita..." he groaned, swiftly moving his hips.

My hands combed through his short hair as once again my pleasure took away my ability to talk. My toes pointed towards the ceiling, as I moaned. My eyes were closed from the heart pulsing pleasure and my chest moved frantically.

Damn did I miss getting fucked like this. It was hardcore, yet it was also loving and tender. It was everything you wanted from a man.

"Harder..." we're the only words I was able to mutter. I was almost there.

Bryson increased his pace. He moved feverishly working up a sweat. So much so that we both slipped off the couch. He landed on his back and I landed on top of him. We both laughed, looking at each other.

"Oh, my God. Got carried away. Are you okay?" He asked, pushing a strand of my hair way.

"Yeah I'm good. It's okay. I'm not crushing you am I?"

"Never. You feel good on top."

"Yeah?" I arched an eyebrow and began stroking his stiffness behind me. He groaned and arched his back.

"Don't tease me." He muttered.

"How bad do you want it?"

"Bad."

"Yeah?"

"Yeah, baby. Please fuck me."

I grinned and sat on his hard cock. I moaned once more as he stretched me out. Holding his shoulders, I rhythmically rolled my hips, riding him.

"Goddamn," he muttered, holding my ass. He lightly slapped it and I giggled.

"Keith was a idiot for letting you go. I fucking love your curves."

"Yeah?" I gasped. "I'm not a fat slob?"

"No, you're a fucking goddess. Keith is trash. You are a treasure. A gift among men. I love every inch of you."

"Every inch?" I muttered.

He nodded. "Every inch, baby. Every fucking inch. Now come for me." He placed his thumb on my clit and massaged it.

At his words, I felt a spark in my core. I don't usually orgasm on command like that, but it was something in Bryson's husky voice that turned me on. His voice captured me, giving me that extra push to go over the edge. Seconds later, I came again.

Bryson grinned, watching as the pleasure took hold of me. He soon followed, pumping hard inside of me as he came. When he was through he gasped and pushed way a strand of my hair.

"That was amazing."

"It sure was."

"I'm happy that you're finally mine."

"Me too." I grinned, leaning down to kiss him. "Ready for bed?"

"By ready for bed you mean are you ready to go again?"

"You got more in the tank?"

"Rita, I got years stored up for you. Come on let's go." He stood and took me to the bedroom to make love once more.

Chapter 3

I woke up naked, draped over Bryson's naked body. It was the first time I woke up with a smile on my face in a long time. The sex marathon lasted a while and let's just say I lost count how many times I came. Bryson was a fucking machine when I came to the bedroom.

As I shifted in bed, Bryson smiled at me.

"Morning beautiful."

"Hi," I grinned.

"Last night was amazing."

"It sure was."

He kissed me and pushed my dangling red hair back.

"Breakfast?" He asked.

"Yes, please. Coffee too?"

"You got it. You stay in bed, naked. I plan on taking you once more this morning."

I grinned and could already feel the excitement of another round of heart pounding sex with Bryson.

Bryson put on an pair of shorts and left the bedroom, leaving me alone I bed.

As I got comfortable, I found the controller and turned it on the news. Half paying attention, I search for my phone and found it in my sweatpants pocket. Turning it on, I discovered multiple missed calls and texts from Keith. My heart dropped the moment I saw it. I quickly turned to the first text seeing him begging for me to come home, saying that he was sorry for the way things were. He wants things to go back to normal. I felt a lump in my throat.

Had I cheated on him, I questioned.

Bryson returned with two cups of coffee in his hands and frowned the moment he saw my face.

"What's wrong."

"It's Keith. He was sorry about last night. He wants me to go back to him."

"Oh…" Bryson sat on the bed and looked down. "What does that mean?"

"I'm not sure. I mean, did I just cheat on him? God, was last night a mistake?"

Bryson shook his head. "I didn't think it was. Keith is a dumbass, who didn't know a good thing and when it was gone, he's now begging for it back."

"I know, but Keith and I have history."

"So do we." Bryson replied. "I'm tried of you getting hurt Rita."

"I know. Ugh, I don't know what to do."

"Whatever you decide I will support."

I open my eyes wide. "Really?"

"Yes, granted if you chose Keith, it would break my heart, but I wouldn't hate you for it. I love you. You're my soulmate, Rita. I know that we will be together. I'll be there. No matter what."

I grinned and looked at my phone as another text came in from Keith begging for me to come home. I then looked at Bryson who stood confident, smiling at me.

Right there I realized the choice was easy. It was there for me all along.

"I choose you." I replied.

Bryson's eyes opened wide. "Really?"

"Yes, as you said. We're soulmates. I might not have seen it before, but now I know. We were meant to be." I leaned forward and kissed him. "I now know that you love me and we are meant to be together forever."

"Ah, Rita. I love you." He kissed me back and placed his forehead on mine. "I promise, till the end of days, I will love you." He whispered.

From that day, Bryson kept his promise to me and from that day, I learned who my true love was.

Always There
Chapter 1

"Please, just give me another week. I promise I'll get your money." I begged my landlord.

"I've given you three months to pay me. At this point you're almost considered a squatter."

"Please, I know I've been late, but my son and I need this space. We can't be homeless. This is the only affordable place in the city

"I'm sorry, but I don't run a charity. I expect your stuff out of the apartment by the end of the day. By then the locks will be changed and anything left in the place would be thrown away. I'm sorry, Katrina."

My jaw dropped and I could feel the tears well in my eyes. I tried to stay strong for my son, but it was getting a harder by the second.

The landlord left the apartment and my four year old son, Ty appeared behind me. He had similar features as me, with dark skin, a big nose and large brown eyes. He got his lanky build from his deadbeat father, whose God knows where right now.

"What happened mommy?"

I sniffed, holding back from breaking down. "We have to move."

"Move?"

"Yes, leave."

"But this is our home."

"I know baby, but mommy can't afford it."

"Where are we going to stay?"

"I don't know. We are going to get a hotel room and then perhaps drive to grandma's house."

"Grandma's? You don't like her."

I sighed. "It's not that I don't like her. It's just that grandma and me don't see eye to eye. I'm not happy to be going to her house either, but if we don't go, we'd be living outside on the streets. We must stay with her."

My son nodded.

"I love you." I reassured.

" I love mommy."

I smiled and kissed his forehead. "How about you go and make a bag of toys to take with us."

"I want all of them!"

"No, baby. We must leave some stuff here as grandma won't take all of it. We just going to take a few clothes and toys."

"Okay." He slumped his shoulders and walked away.

I closed my eyes and I could feel the tears roll down my cheeks. I had no idea where I was going. I took a deep breath and then wiped my tears away. Now wasn't the time to be upset. My son needed me to be strong. I needed to be strong.

Walking into the bedroom, I grabbed several bags, and then stuffed as many clothes as I could inside my suitcases. As I packed my phone went off, seeing it was my best friend from high school, I answered it.

"Hey, Liam, I can't talk right now."

"Oh, okay. Sorry to bother you. I was just calling to catch up. I can call back later."

"Yes, that would be great."

"Okay..." he paused and then asked, "Is everything alright?"

"Yeah, everything is fine. Why do you ask?"

"I've known you since the 10th grade. I know when something is up. Tell me what's wrong. Perhaps I can help."

I sighed and rubbed my temples. "I just got evicted and have till the end of the day to leave."

"Seriously?"

"Yes, like I said, I have a lot to get done between now and then. Can I talk to you later?"

"Wait, do you have a place to stay?"

"I'm getting a hotel and then driving to my mom's place."

"But you hate your mom."

"Don't remind me."

"Do you have anywhere else to stay?"

"Not for the long term. Most of our friends have kids and no space for me and Ty to stay."

"I could take you in."

"Liam, I don't want to be a bother."

"You're never a bother to me. Please, I have a three bedroom home and two spare rooms with en-suite bathrooms. That's plenty of space."

"I can't pay rent right now though. I barely have enough money as it is."

"Don't worry about it. Just pay me when you can. Seriously, please come and stay with me."

The way he said stay with me made me tremble. I always had a thing for Liam, but never knew how to tell him. Unlike me, Liam had his life together. He went to college, got a job in engineering, and owned his own house. Me on the other hand, hopped from job to job and got knocked up by an asshole. If there was a score in life, mine would be zero.

I sighed, and thought about my options. Ty was a handful, and as a toddler, he could be a lot to non-parents. I didn't want to burden Liam with him either.

"What about Ty? He can be a lot."

"I love Ty . You've seen me and him together before. We might even go to the park tomorrow, just to give you a break."

I bit my lip as the option to stay with Liam was sounding better.

"What do you say?" He asked.

I sighed and shrugged. "Sure. I'll stay with you. It's only temporary. Like I said, I don't want to be a burden."

"You're never a burden to me, Katrina. You and Ty are always welcome. I really care for you both. I'd do anything for y'all."

The tone of his voice made my stomach tie in knots. I questioned if he too had feelings, but quickly dismissed it as I reminded myself that we were just friends.

"Thanks, Liam."

"Anytime. Do you need help moving?"

"No, I'll see you at your place."

"Okay see you soon."

I hung up with Liam, wondering what I was getting into. Liam was a good friend, but was he something more now that I will be living with him.

Chapter 2

We arrived at Liam's two hours later. Liam lived in a brick ranch home in a quiet neighborhood. Honestly, I was envious of where Liam lived. it was the ideal neighborhood for Ty to be in. There were kids playing outside on the streets, the neighborhood was cleaned and people waved at you. The apartment I stayed in was unsafe, and wasn't the best environment for me or Ty.

When I arrived, Liam was waiting outside. He was wearing a basketball T-shirt and shorts. Liam was a foot taller than me, and had an athletic build, with pale skin and shaggy reddish brown hair.

I hopped out of my car first and then helped Ty out of his booster seat in the back. Liam walked up towards me and greeted me.

"Hey, Katrina."

"Hi, Liam." I gave him a hug and rubbed his back. "Thanks for taking me in."

"I will always be there for you." He gave me a light smile before looking at Ty . "What's up Ty ." He held out a fist and Ty immediately bumped it.

"Hi!" Ty grinned.

"Listen, I bought some pizza for dinner. How does that sound?"

"Pizza?" Ty looked at me for approval and I nodded.

"Pizza sounds great. You didn't need to do that, Liam."

"Nonsense. You needed a break. I figured y'all were hungry. I'll get your bags, y'all can head inside." Liam, grabbed the bags from me and Ty and then ushered us inside.

At the entrance of the ranch house was the living room, and at the far end of the living area was the dining room and kitchen. Towards my left, down the hall, were the bedrooms.

From the distance, I could see two boxes of pizza sitting on the dining room table. Liam followed me inside, placing the suitcases near the entrance of the door.

"Whose hungry?" He grinned.

"I am!" Ty yelled, bouncing up and down.

Liam grinned and held, Ty's hand leading him to the table. I grinned watching the two interact. It was strange because even though Liam wasn't his father, he surely acted like it. How I wished things were different.

Dinner with Liam went great. It was great seeing Ty smile again, as most of the day, he was down after losing the apartment and a lot of his toys. Liam was a godsend as he managed to lift everyone's moods. After pizza, we had a dance party and ice cream, making a bad day into a great night.

After tucking Ty into bed, I found Liam in the living room watching tv on the sofa.

"How is he?" Liam asked.

"Better now. Thank you for taking us in." I replied, sitting next to him on the sofa.

"No problem."

"Seriously. I know I can't pay you back now, but I will."

"I trust you." Liam grinned. "In the meantime, how about a drink? Ease that tension?"

"Yes, please."

Liam grinned and grabbed a bottle of tequila from the nearby bar in the kitchen.

"Tequila? This still is your drink of choice right?"

"Yes, oh I need it."

Liam grinned and prepared my drink, adding two ice cubes into a glass and pouring the liquor inside.

"Here you go," he replied, handing me a glass. "Two fingers of tequila with two ice cubes. Just how you like it."

"Thank you. I'm amazed you remember those small details about me."

"I remember everything about you." He grinned.

That smile sent a shiver up my spine. What was this feeling coming over me?

Taking a few breaths I managed to calm myself. I took a sip of the alcohol and moaned from the taste.

"Perfect."

"You like it?"

"Of course." I winked. I took another sip and then turned my attention to a movie that Liam was watching.

"What are you watching?" I asked.

"It's a new movie on Netflix. Its like this spy thriller, where they have to catch a Russian spy. I can change it, if you don't want to watch it."

"Oh, no I like action. Leave it on, I'll follow the plot."

He nodded and resumed watching the movie. As we watched the movie, I found myself scooting closer and closer to Liam. Inches apart, I placed my head on his shoulder. I felt his body get tense, but then he relaxed, placing an arm around me. We both quietly cuddling until Liam paused the movie.

"Hey, Katrina, can I ask you a question?"

"Sure..."

"While I don't mind you guys staying, I have to know. Is there something between us?"

"What do you mean?"

"I can't describe it. I don't want to call it fate, but I've had a crush on you for some time, and I always wanted to tell you, but our lives always got in the way, however now that you're here, I feel like I can't keep it a secret any more. I like you Katrina. You and Ty mean so much to me."

"Liam...where is this coming from? Why didn't you tell me before?"

He shrugged. "I was too scared to say something, but I realized today, that being with you and Ty was wonderful. Between having dinner and our little dance party, I couldn't keep a smile off my face. I want every day to be like that."

"Liam, you and I both know that stuff doesn't exist. Life doesn't work that way. Life ain't a fairy tale."

"It should. We both deserve to be happy. I want both of you in my life. I want you to be my happy ending."

"Liam, I'm sorry, I like you too, but..."

"But what?"

"For starters, Ty and I are both black, you're white, have you thought about..."

"I don't care what your skin color is, damn anyone who judges us. My parents taught me to value someone's personality over skin color, and you and Ty both have wonderful personalities. You both are amazing."

"Yes, but how do I know this isn't just something spur in the moment. Yeah, we have history, but taking us in is a lot. Things could change and..."

"I don't care about the changes. Now, five years from now, ten years from now, it doesn't matter. How I feel about you, won't change. I won't change. I love you." He admitted.

My heart did a 360 as soon as he said those words. My skin felt warm, and I unexpectedly felt lightheaded.

He loved me, I repeated in my head.

I wanted to say it back, but strangely my lips felt glued together at the moment.

Liam leaned forward as if he was expecting a kiss, and I hesitated. I wanted this yet something held me back. I was afraid of what the future would bring. Between my ex and being evicted, I did not want to feel helpless again if our relationship fizzled out. It may be a happy ending for him, but it could be my nightmare.

I leaned back and shook my head.

"I'm sorry, Liam, I can't do this."

His jaw dropped as he watched me get up and walk away.

"Katrina, wait...I'm sorry."

"It's okay. It was a mistake coming here. Perhaps it would be better if I stayed with my mother."

"Katrina..." Liam begged, but I was already leaving, heading back down to Ty's room.

Laying down in the bed I felt like such a fool.

Chapter 3

I didn't get any sleep. After making my decision with Liam, I still felt bad about it. I questioned if it was the right choice. I liked Liam. He was a good guy, he was great with Ty and not once had he let me down. Why was I so afraid of being with him?

I shuffled in bed and turned to watch Ty sleep peacefully. I smiled at my son and softly brushed his hair.

Perhaps I was overthinking it. Liam liked me. I liked him. I wasn't a fortune teller and couldn't see the future. Perhaps things won't be as bad. Liam is a good man, who loves both me and my son, but do I love him?

I hesitated and sat up in the bed. I couldn't decide, but I had to answer the question. I had to know. I crept out of the bedroom towards Liam's room. His door was closed and I knocked it.

Liam opened the door wide eyed.

"Katrina, is everything okay?"

"Is this love real?" I blurted.

"Katrina...I..."

"Just answer the question. Is this love real or are you just saying these things?"

"Katrina, my love for you is boundless. It's unwavering and strong. Words can only go so far, but I plan to spend the rest of my life, proving to you how much I love you ..."

Before he could say another word, I let my emotions take over. I no longer worried about tomorrow and just focused on today. All I wanted was him in that moment and I let myself have him. Leaping into his arms, I passionately kissed him, taking his breath away.

He gasped and pushed me away. His eyes were wide and his chest moved sporadically.

"Katrina..."

"I'm sorry, was that to much?"

"No, it was perfect. You're perfect."

I smiled and he dragged me closer to his lips once more. His kiss was soft and emotional. It felt like years of pent-up feelings were released all in one kiss. In one kiss, I felt weightless. In one kiss, I felt safe. In one kiss, I felt love. There was no denying his feelings. His kiss said it all.

"I love you," I admitted. If finally felt good to say those words. Those words scared me at first, but now I finally know. I finally know that I am in love with Liam Oliver.

"I know you do. I will always be there. Understand?"

I nodded holding the back of his head as we embraced each other.

"I don't want to sleep alone. Can I sleep with you?" I whispered.

"Are you sure?"

"I've never been more sure of something in my life."

He grinned and picked me up, he carried me towards the bed and laid me down. He followed, laying on top of me, kissing my lips and neck. I moaned softly as our passionate fires ignited. My legs arched and wrapped around his torso, dragging him closer to me. Like a spider, I snared him in my web and I didn't plan on letting him go.

He groaned, as he ground his body on top of mine. I felt him get harder. His thick cock rubbed against my thigh as our excitement grew. My hands lowered towards the hem of his sweatpants, and I grasped his throbbing length. Slowly, I stroked him, and he moaned my name.

His head was buried in the nook of my neck. My name was at the tip of his tongue as I pleasured him.

"Oh, Katrina..." he muttered. His hands reached down towards my pajamas bottoms and he pulled them down. I moaned as the cool air collided with my wet core. I soon felt his finger inside me and I gasped, feeling it jerk back and forth.

"I want to taste you..." Liam muttered as he slid down towards my crotch. With me on the edge of the bed, Liam sat on his knees as he pleasured me. His tongue slipped in and out of my folds, making me cry out in pleasure. The way Liam serviced me was different. The simulation was different. He was different.

It wasn't just the way he touched me. It was the way he moaned my name. It was the way he held me. It was the way worshipped me like a queen. For those mere seconds, I felt how he truly cared about me. It was breathtaking and awe inspiring. I came within a few minutes, and was left gasping for air.

Liam grinned, looking down at me.

"Do you want more?" He asked.

"Don't tease me." I retorted.

"I would never. Let me get a condom."

He searched for a rubber in the drawer of his night stand, and brought out the small package.

"Nice to know you're prepared. Get a lot of women in your bedroom?"

"No, I've been holding on to them for a while. Don't worry it's not expired. I checked."

"That's good to know." I giggled.

He grinned and he removed the rest of his clothes. My eyes fluttered as I took in his athletic frame. Fuck was he sexy.

"I got these condoms in hope that the woman, I've loved will come knocking on my door. You just did and now I get to celebrate doing the thing I've wished to do since grade school."

"You've had a crush on me for that long?"

"Yeah, baby. I knew you were for me the moment I saw you across the cafeteria. I didn't have the courage to say something then, but now that I have you, I don't plan on ever letting you go." He unwrapped the foil wrapper with one hand and slipped out the white condom. Laying there, watching him roll the latex over his hard shaft made me tremble.

As he approached me, our eyes connected. It felt like he was staring right into my soul.

"Are you sure you want this?"

"I do, Liam. I love you. I want you so bad."

He grinned and climbed on top of me. Slowly he entered, me stretching me out. I moaned as a new wave of pleasure took hold.

"How is that?"

"Fucking amazing." I grinned.

He smiled back at me and kissed me gingerly. Slowly, he began to thrust gradually increasing his speed. I moaned, holding on to his ass. He moved rhythmically with me, back and forth we went, sharing each other. Both of us were in harmony, singing our praises as our pleasures took over. He felt good. Really good.

We shifted in the bed and I was on top. I quickly tossed of my tank top, as our steamy session continued. He held my waist looking up at me.

"I fucking love your body."

"Yeah?"

"Everything about it is so damn sexy. I love how our two skin colors blend together, nothing compares. My pale skin, your soft brown skin, It's picture perfect, like an evening sunset. I've dreamed of this moment, and now that it's here, I don't want it to end. Fuck..." he groaned. His thumb brushed over my taut nipple, making me groaned. I closed my eyes as my body shuddered from the sensation.

"How does that feel?" I asked.

"Really good?"

"Oh, baby."

I smiled looking at his pale hands cupping my dark mounds. His eyes were wide and I could tell he was fascinated by every inch of my curves.

Reaching down, I held his chin, and gasped, "I want you to come for me."

"Right now?" He asked.

"Yes, baby. I want to feel you at your peak. Please come."

He grinned and held my waist tightly. He groaned, thrusting into me harder. From the increase movement, I moaned and tighten my grip on his body. My legs shook as I felt my own pleasure grow. Seconds later, he let out a loud grunt and exhaled as he came into the condom. When he was through, I held his face cheeks, peering into his eyes.

"That was wonderful."

"Yeah, it was."

I leaned forward and kissed him. "I love you."

"I love you too." He whispered.

After rolling off of him, he held me close and we both looked up at the ceiling, breathing heavily from our loving affair.

"Are you sure about this?" I asked.

"About us?" He questioned.

I nodded.

"I'm very sure. This is all I've ever wanted in life. I promise, I will always be there, okay?"

"Okay." I grinned.

Liam kissed me once more and held me close. As I laid there, I still had my doubts, but over time, Liam proved to me he was true to his word. He truly was always there. Whenever I needed him, he was there. Whenever I was down, he was there. He was there for the bad and the good. He really did love me and Ty.

From that night, our relationship grew, into something serious. A year later he proposed to me, soon after we got married, got a bigger house, and had two more kids.

This wasn't the life I expected when I got evicted, but I'm glad it happened to me. I got my fairy tale ending, and I couldn't be more happier.

The First Date

Sharron applied her cherry red lipstick on her lips with haste. She knew she should have left twenty minutes later, but her mom took her time to arrive at her apartment to watch her son, making her late for her date. Dating while being a single parent was impossible.

Looking in the car mirror, she sighed. Judging by what she was wearing, it looked like she didn't even own an iron. She was wearing a brown sweater with blue jeans. Along with the pants, she paired them with a pair of brown knee high riding boots. She figured, the outfit would be perfect for the cool winter afternoon at the Virginia Beach oceanfront. She growled loudly jostling the end of her sweater trying to get the multiple wrinkles out.

After one last glance in the mirror, she adjusted the tie on her ebony curls, and smiled. "You got this Sharron. You have been video chatting with him for a month. He's cute, funny, and was great with Deshawn when you video called him. This should be a breeze."

After a deep breath, she exited the vehicle and walked inside the restaurant. Her date chose a fine dining seafood eatery that was on the boardwalk. Past the front door, was a large fish tank with multiple colored fish. Around the walls, was a nautical theme, with anchors, oars, ship wheels, and buoys. The tables had white pressed cloths draping down the edges. Every staff member matched in a pressed white shirt, tucked in a pair of black trousers. After telling the host she was meeting someone, she spotted her date, Brad Williams. He was sitting at a table near the window watching the sunset and the waves on the beach.

Wow, he's fine as hell.

Brad was the definition of handsome. He had short brown hair, a perfectly shaved scruffy beard, and a fantastic smile. Like Sharron, he wore a sweater, but his was grey and he wore brown khakis with boat shoes. His sleeves were rolled up to his forearms, displaying his chiseled physique. When he noticed her walking in, his smile grew larger. He stood up and gave her a hug.

"Hello Sharron. You look absolutely stunning," he greeted her with a kiss on her cheek. His voice was powerful and in a British accent. She blushed at the feeling of his lips on her soft skin. From the reaction, she looked down and played with her sweater cuffs.

"Oh, thank you. You look handsome as well. I like your sweater. It's so sharp!" she said, rubbing her hand down the wool fiber. As she ran her fingers across the fabric, they graced his hard pectorals and her fingers jolted back as if they were struck by a bolt of lightning.

He pulled out the chair for her, and she took her seat. "Such a gentleman."

"You know us Brits. We've invented chivalry."

"No one wonder James Bond gets all the women."

Brad chucked and opened his menu.

"How is Deshawn?" he asked, flipping through the menu.

"Good? Naturally, he wanted to come, you know seven year old's. I had to explain that this dinner was for grownups only. Did Mary put up a fight when you told her about the date?" She asked, grabbing the glass of water in front of her and taking a sip. Looking across to Brad, he nodded.

"Yes, she did. Before, I left, she sneaked away from the nanny and belted herself in the car. I had to promise her, that on our next date, I'll bring her along to meet you and Deshawn." Sharron choked on her water as it spilled out of her mouth.

"Oh!" Brad grabbed his napkin and dapped her face, drying the escaped liquid. "I'm terribly sorry."

"No, no, it's fine." Sharron could feel her cheek grow warm again. "I'm sorry, it's just that I haven't been on a formal date for some time. That was a perfect entry for me to flirt and say something, like who said you were getting a second date, but I completely ruined it with my inability to drink water."

Brad laughed and refolded his cloth napkin.

"I think you're doing okay so far. And to answer your question from before, I know I'm getting a second date, because I'm a natural charmer. Not to mention, if you denied me a second date, I would blame it all on you and tell my daughter about it. Therefore, making you my daughter's public enemy number one. She probably hate you for the rest of her life."

"You wouldn't!"

Brad shrugged. "Your honor would just be a casualty of love."

"How rude! You see, this is why we separated from the British in the first place. I'm glad we won." She crossed her arms and rose her eyebrows.

"Oh, that didn't take too long. You Yanks always throwing that blasted war in our face." Brad sat up straight and held a tight lipped smile. The two stared at each other in silence until Sharron broke out laughing. Brad joined in, clutching his side.

"God, Brad I love your humor."

"I love everything about you."

Sharron gave him a sideways glance.

What in the hell did he mean by that?, she thought.

The duo fell silent once more, their eyes glued to the menu, until Brad cleared his throat.

"Do you see anything on the menu that you'd like?"

"I'm not sure. A glass of wine wouldn't be so bad to start?" Sharron flipped the menu to the wine section and her eyes grew wide. "Oh wow, there's so many of them."

"Do you mind if I choose?"

"Please go right ahead." Brad nodded and reviewed the wine menu. Watching his blue eyes scan the menu, Sharron attempted to hide a smile. She re-crossed her legs and adjusted her outfit, attempting to sit in a more sultry position.

"Well the secret on picking out a good wine is..." Brad looked away from the menu and his eyes were drawn to Sharron. Like a moth to the flame, he was attracted to every inch of her. He shuddered, and his palms became sweaty. In attempt to cover his fault, he coughed and readjusted his pants. "Excuse me," Brad grabbed his water and took a long sip.

Sharron did nothing but smile, knowing exactly what she did.

"Forgive me. My mouth was parched. As I was saying, the secret on picking out a good wine is to pair it with the entrée. I'm feeling like oysters to start, then perhaps the halibut as the entrée, my wine pairing would have to be a glass of the Woodsong Chardonnay. It's simply brilliant."

"Oh all of that sounds good. I'll have the same."

Brad rose his eyes and grinned. He looked away and flagged down their waiter. As Brad ordered the food, Sharron looked out the window, watching the waves crash into the beach.

"Wow, would you look at that sunset. It's beautiful." Sharron stared at the orange and red star slowly dipping below the blue sea. The way the light reflected off the waves was stunning and picturesque, like an artist's mosaic painting.

"The sunset does not compare to your beauty." Brad admitted.

Sharron turned back to Brad. The restaurant felt like it was one hundred degrees, as she began to sweat. Fanning herself, she giggled loudly.

"Oh Brad. Stop it." Sharron grinned lightly slapping his arm. As she pulled away, Brad caught her arm. She rose her eyes up, not expecting him to grab her wrist, however, once his large ivory hands covered her small ebony wrist, she melted like butter. He slowly massaged her wrist. The way he pressed her skin in a circular motion made her want to moan out loud. "Oh Brad, that feels good. Could you keep it up?"

"Yeah, but better yet..." Brad got out of his chair and walked around her. "May I?" He asked pointing to her shoulders.

Sharron hesitated, but then nodded. "Yes, that's fine."

Brad grinned and then Sharron felt his masculine rough hands touch feminine soft shoulders. Like a professional, he began to kneed her deltoid muscles.

"Brad wait, are you allowed to do this? This is a fancy restaurant and..."

"Shhhh... just relax. Your shoulders are so tense. As for the restaurant, they could piss off." Her mouth dropped at his admission, but soon, she forgot all about his bravado. She was lost in a state of bliss from the massage. As his fingers danced across her shoulders, she moaned softly and dropped her head down allowing him to have greater access. "How does that feel?"

"Amazing."

"Your shoulders are so tense. What's wrong?"

"What isn't wrong. The stress of being a single parent. Since Malik walked out, it's just been Deshawn and me. I haven't had a night for myself in ages." Sharron rolled her neck once more enjoying his magic fingers on her skin.

"I understand. After Mary's mum passed, life has been hard for us too. Even though it's been three years, Mary misses her mum everyday." Brad stopped giving Sharron a massage and took a seat across from her. His eyes, which were once filled with light, were dark. His fists clenched and his body grew ridged. Sharron disliked the frown that hung low on his face. Reaching out to him, she rubbed his fists. Slowly, his fingers relaxed, and she held his hand.

"Every time I hear about your wife. I feel like I'm going to cry. I'm so sorry that you lost her. I can't imagine the pain you felt from losing her."

"It's quite alright. Losing her in the airplane explosion was sudden, but I'm happy she died painlessly though." Brad rubbed the back of his neck.

"She would have been proud of the father that you've become. Your daughter is beautiful."

Brad cracked a smile and rubbed her hand. The waiter returned with two crystal wine goblets and a basket of bread. After popping the wine cork off, he elegantly poured the white wine in the glass. Once he was done, he placed the bottle in a silver tin.

"Thank you Thomas." Our waiter smiled at Brad and walked back towards the kitchen. "Cheers," Brad grinned holding up his wine.

"Cheers." She replied colliding her glass with his. After taking a sip of the smooth velvety wine she moaned. "Oh, this is good." She took another sip and detected hints of lemon and vanilla in the wine. Placing down her wine glass, Sharron reached for a piece of bread, but her hand awkwardly smashed into Brad's as he attempted to grab bread as well. The two laughed and pulled their hands back.

"You go first."

"Thank you," Sharron grinned, taking a piece of warm bread from the pile. Brad followed taking a piece for himself. While Sharron buttered her roll, Brad halved it and ate the soft filling. "You don't like eating the entire roll?"

"I only like the soft filling of the bread. I can't stand the hard crust. Since I was a boy, not once have I eaten the edges of the bread."

"That's the best part. The hard crispness of the bread. The satisfying crunch it makes as it swirls in your mouth. You should try it."

"Are you sure?"

Sharron laughed and nodded. Brad ripped the edge off the bread and stared at it. He slowly placed the crust in his mouth and chewed.

"So?"

"It's different."

"Different as in a good thing?"

"Yes. I'm actually enjoying it." He smirked and popped another piece of bread in his mouth. " Who knew dating you would be adventurous." The two laughed once more. "How is Deshawn doing in school?"

"He's excited as usual. I swear I only feed him cereal and orange juice in the morning, but the kid bounces around like I've feed him pure sugar and coffee. He has more energy than I could ever handle. Does Mary like her private school?"

"I'm not sure. She doesn't talk to me much about it. It's hard to get her to open up. She was a lot more open with her mum than me. I think she's getting bullied in school."

"What makes you think that?" Brad shrugged and took another sip of his wine.

"I've spotted her crying on several occasions. Whenever I drop her off, none of the kids speak to her. They look at her as if she has a plague. All I want to do is help my little girl, but I don't know how."

Sharron nodded. "Have you tried talking to her about it?"

"I've tried setting up a time to meet, but something always comes up with work. I only have enough hours in the day to see her, before she has to go to bed. I want to spend more time with my daughter, but I can't."

"You must find the time. Skip a few board meetings show up late once in a while. Jobs come and go, but you only get one daughter. Talk to her. Talk her teachers. Talk to her classmates. Learn the situation and then act upon it."

"That's good advice. You're a good mum."

Sharron shrugged in response and nibbled on another piece of bread.

"Well don't think of me as the perfect parent, because I'm not. I know the feeling of being helpless with your child. I love Deshawn to death, but he has this aggressive nature. Last year, he was sent to the principal's office for fighting so many times. He even got suspended for a week for his behavior. I've done all that I could do. He's a sweet kid, I just don't know what to do to decrease his anger."

"Have you tried putting him in sports?"

"Oh, I'm not a big fan of sports."

"I know, but it sounds like your son needs an outlet to divert his anger towards something. Like football."

"Oh, I don't like football. It's too violent."

"Not that American rubbish. I'm talking about what you would call soccer. A true team sport of endurance and perseverance. Your son is the perfect age to start to play. I played when I was his age. Even played at club level until I got my knee injury. Football, is a team sport at its core. Every player needs each other to win. Your son would benefit by playing on a team. I could teach him how to play if you wanted me too."

"That would be nice, except I'm still not sure if I owe you a second date yet." She smirked and winked. Brad grinned at her flirtatious smile.

"Oh, I see what you did there. You're a lot more convincing on the second go."

Sharron giggled and then watched the waiter carry a plate of steamed oysters towards them. "Here comes our food."

"It's about bloody time. I was about to go back there and cook it myself."

Once the plate of the warmed shellfish was put on the table, Brad indicated for Sharron to grab the first oyster. Sharron squeezed a lemon on top of the oyster and added a dash of hot sauce on her meat. With a fork, she slid the slimy gummy seafood into her mouth. Tasting the oyster was like tasting the ocean. She grinned from the salty meat.

Brad had the same reaction after taking a sip of his wine. "How's the oyster?"

"Delicious. These are the best oysters I've ever tasted. Not to mention the wine is a perfect choice."

"I'm glad to hear it," He said, pouring more wine for Sharron.

"Thank you."

The sound of chewing and forks scratching plates were only heard as the couple enjoyed the dozen oysters. After placing the last oyster shell on the tray, Brad grinned at Sharron.

"That certainly hit the spot."

"It sure did." Sharron sighed and looked out the window.

"What's wrong?" Brad asked, rubbing her hand.

"Malik would have never brought me to a nice restaurant like this. His idea of fine dining was going to the local bar and ordering a steak. This however-" She turned back and held his hand. Her russet thumb, rubbed his pale skinned palm in a circular motion. "This date is better than I've imagined. I can't wait to see what you have in store for the second date."

Brad grinned, "It will be even better than this."

The waiter took away their plates from their appetizer and placed two small spoons of lemon sherbet. Sharron tilted her head and lifted up the spoon.

"Ice cream before dinner? Is this restaurant ran by my son or something?"

"Oh, no, it's to cleanse the palate." Sharron gave him another sideways glance. "Trust me. Just try it."

Sharron placed the cold treat and in her mouth and was surprised that Brad was right. Her mouth no longer tasted fishy, it was cold and tasted of fresh lemon.

"Huh, well I'll be. I guess you were right."

"I'm always right," he amused taking a sip of his wine. The waiter turned with two dishes of fish along with plates of steamed vegetables and mashed potatoes. Sharron's mouth watered once more looking at the wonderfully prepared halibut. The rectangular white filet was grilled to perfection. "I hope you enjoy your fish.

"Oh I'm sure I will." Using her fork, she cut through the flaky meat with ease. Upon the first bite, she moaned savoring the complex flavors of the fish.

"It's brilliant, yeah?"

"Yes! Wow, I've never tasted fish like this." She forked another piece of halibut and placed it in her mouth. Halfway through her fish, she moved on to the sides of veggies and potato mash. After forking a carrot, she dipped the vegetable into the mash potatoes and ate it.

"You dip your food into the potato mash as well?" He asked copying her motions.

"Yes? I always thought I was the only one."

"It appears that's not the case. I like doing it because it reminds me of me mum's shepherds pie."

The two laughed and then fell silent once more enjoying their meal. Sharron made sure her plate was empty before placing the fork down. She even scooped up the fish gravy with a piece of bread, just to taste every last bit of her entrée.

"Wow, I'm stuffed. I think that's the first time, I've ever finished a whole meal by myself."

"I guess you don't have any room for dessert."

"The only dessert I can stomach right now is-"

"Crème brûlée," they said together.

"Took the words right out of my mouth," Sharron smirked.

"It's because I remember everything about you."

Brad signaled the waiter and he disappeared in the kitchen. Soon the waiter brought out two crème brûlée's and placed it in front of the couple. Sharon beamed and was at a lost of words staring at the crystallized sugar treat.

"Go ahead, dig in." With a smile, she cracked the sugar and gathered a large portion of the filling on her spoon. After a bite, she moaned at the fluffy vanilla flavor of the dessert.

"How is it?"

"Amazing."

The clatter of spoons where heard until both of the ceramic dishes were empty.

Once Brad finished his dessert he rubbed his stomach and grinned, "Now I'm full."

"I've been stuffed for the last five minutes. I have no idea where this food is going to go. Hopefully not my butt."

"I've always liked a curvy woman."

"Hey! You're not doing anything to help your chances for a second date."

"What? I thought I already had a second date in the bag."

"No, I just wanted a free meal out of this. I got it. You do know that overconfidence is how the British lost the war."

"Bloody hell, I thought we were done making fun of my home country."

Sharron winked and shrugged. "Oh, there's more where that comes from. Just wait for the jokes that I have on our second date."

"You mean..."

"You better get ready for round two."

"I wouldn't have it any other way." Brad grinned.

There were many other dates after this one, however nothing ever compared to the first. To Brad and Sharron, this first date was the start of their relationship. It was the spark of their love. This first date was the groundwork for their everlasting romance. Date after date, the two fell for each other. Their relationship grew, their two families became one, and they lived happily ever after.

The End

Runaway With Me
Chapter 1

Fall of 1961

Jane didn't know what to expect when she went to the dance social with her brother, Fred. During the fall, her small liberal arts college in North Carolina became desegregated and fourteen black students attended the college. She'd never seen a black person on campus, but she'd heard what others had said about them. In the prior week, the biggest rumor on campus was that the college was allowing blacks to attend the social. Of course the campus was in uproar, but she wasn't bothered by the idea.

Personally she never had a problem with black people and she didn't understand why there was so much aggression about her school being desegregated. In her mind, blacks were still humans, and should be treated with the same respect that she would want to be treated with. Well, that is how she interpreted her teachings as a child. Her brother must have learned something different as his thoughts on blacks aligned with most of the white population in the south..

She wished her brother shared the same wisdom. He thought that all black people were some sort of plague that was infecting everything that was right about America. Every time he'd see a black person on tv or hear one on the radio he'd make a horrible racist comment.

It sickened her, but she never had the courage to stand up to him. He played football at the college and was an incredible athlete. Unlike him, she was a skinny scholar and got into the college with her brain, not her brawn.

Walking into the gymnasium, the band was playing an upbeat swing song. Even though the school was desegregated, you couldn't tell based on the way that half of the gym was filled with black people and the other white. It was like there was an invisible rope separating the two groups.

Jane straighten the wrinkles in her dress and followed her brother who met with his group of friends.

"Bill, how you doing?" Fred asked, shaking his hand.

"Been better. Can you believe that they would let *them* attend this dance? This is my senior year, and I have to share it with negros." Bill replied, nodding to the group of black people dancing.

Jane turned and watched the group of black people dance. Compared to her white peers the group looked to be the better dancers as she watched with astonishment. She was lost in her own thoughts before she heard her brother curse underneath his breath.

"It's a shame." Fred replied, "you know my father didn't die in World War II for America to go to shit. This wasn't the country he wanted. Who knew that true enemy wasn't the Nazis in Germany, it was here in our own country. Perhaps they had it right about eliminating inferior races."

Bill laughed, but Jane frowned, and slapped her brother's shoulder.

"Father would be ashamed to hear you say such a thing. You and I both know he despised the Nazis."

"Dammit Jane, what's got you flustered? Huh?" Fred asked. "What you sympathize with those people?"

"I don't know what I think, but I do know that they deserve some respect. Since they step foot on this campus, all they've received is hatred from others."

"Ha, who would have thought that Fred Williams' sister is a *negro lover*." Bill mocked.

Fred's eyebrows rose and his cheeks became flushed with color.

"She is not!" He snapped.

"Really? Sure sounds like it. Not to mention, she hasn't taken her eyes off them yet."

Fred glared at Jane and grabbed her wrist. She yelped in pain.

"Ouch, Fred, you're hurting me."

"Shut up. You've embarrassed me enough. Go and dance with Bill. Prove to him that your no negro lover."

"I won't. You're such an asshole Fred." Jane cried and ran away from her brother.

"Shit, Jane wait. I'm sorry!" Fred called out, but the damage was done. Jane hated her brother at that moment. Before he could catch up, Jane quickly dashed underneath the bleachers and watched as Fred ran past her attempting to find her.

As Jane wiped her tears away, she heard a voice behind her.

"Ma'am, are you okay?"

Jane jumped to find a tall, athletic black man behind her. He had short hair and wore a grey suit with a red tie and white shirt. He had a gentle smile as he approached her.

"I'm fine." Jane replied, wiping way her tears.

"Are you? I saw the fight with that man. Was that your boyfriend?"

"Brother."

"Oh, families can be tough. I grew up with eight brothers and sisters, with only one bathroom, so you can imagine the fights we got in."

Jane giggled. "Yes, I'm sure the morning fights for bathroom time were intense."

"They were the worst. Well, I'm glad to see you laughing. I am happy to know that I made your night better. Have a good night."

The man backed away before Jane said, "Wait, can I at least get your name?"

"It's Malcom."

"Nice to meet you Malcom, my name is Jane."

"A beautiful name for a beautiful woman."

Jane blushed and looked down at her shoes. "Thank you. I believe I saw you earlier when I walked in the gymnasium. You are a great dancer. I wish I could dance like you."

"Thank you. Dancing isn't hard if you have the right partner."

"Could you perhaps show me how to dance? I've always wanted to learn."

Malcom bit his lip and looked back at the crowd. He shook his head and muttered under his breath before frowning back at Jane. "The fact that I'm talking to you could lead to trouble for me."

"I promise no harm will come to you."

Malcom hesitated. Jane could tell he was in deep thought.

"Listen..." Jane approached Malcom and closed the distance between the two. Malcom's eyes open wide as he took a step back. Jane followed and grabbed his hand. She felt him shiver at her touch, and knew that the very idea of touching a white woman scared him. She tried to make her voice sound sincere as she looked him in his eyes.

"I promise. I'm not like the others. I just want to learn to dance like you, that's all."

Malcom nodded and she noticed a small smile part his lips.

"Okay, I believe you. Which dance move would you like to learn?"

"The one that moves your hips like this?" Jane attempted the move and Malcom laughed.

Jane laughed with him, "What? Don't be rude. Is it that obvious that I don't know what I'm doing?"

"Very," he replied. "Here, let me show you. First rule of dancing is it should be fun. You must be loose. You're too stiff. Shake it off. Like this...." He wiggled his shoulders.

Jane copied his movements, giggling. She felt her heart flutter as she hasn't felt happier in such a long time.

"Good, now spread you legs shoulder length apart, and then shake your hips to the beat."

Jane copied his instructions, and Malcom nodded. "Yeah, that's it. However, remember to follow the beat. You're a bit fast. May I adjust you?" Malcom asked, reaching out to her.

"Yes," Jane replied.

Malcom walked behind her and placed his hands on her hips. As they touched, Jane shivered. She couldn't explain the feeling that she felt as he held her. It was familiar yet foreign. She knew that him touching her was wrong, but all she wanted was his hands on her. Slowly Malcom's hands dragged her closer to his crotch, and the two began moving to the music.

Jane felt his body on hers and felt her stomach twist. There was something about him that gave her butterflies. As they danced close, no longer did they focus on perfecting the dance moves. The two were beyond that. Something else was growing between the pair.

Jane turned around, facing Malcom, and placed her arms around his neck. Their lips were a mere inch apart as they hovered close to each other. Close in proximity, the two locked eyes and were silent as they peered into each other souls. Not a word was spoken, but Jane could tell that they both shared the same emotion.

Jane couldn't explain what was happening to her. It could have been the music or Malcom's bright smile, but she wanted him. It was like she was under some sort of spell. She wanted to kiss him. She wanted to feel his lips upon her own. She wanted Malcom.

As they grew closer together, she heard her brother shout, "Jane! Jane! Where are you?"

Every time her brother called her name, the sound grew closer and closer and Jane knew it was only a matter of time before her brother caught her with Malcom. She feared if she was caught with him, his fate would be a lot worse than hers.

"I have to go. My brother is looking for me."

"Don't go. Stay with me."

"I have too. If my brother catches us..."

Malcom nodded. "I understrand. When can I see you again?"

"Are you free tomorrow? My brother has football practice in the afternoon, you can come to my house and we can dance together again."

"I'd like that. What is your address?'

"1500 Peachtree Avenue. Be there at 3 pm, okay?"

"Okay, I'll see you soon."

"Okay, I'll see you soon, Malcom. Thank you for making a terrible night better."

"For you, I'll do anything."

Jane smiled at his words and felt a warmth in her heart yet again. She waved goodbye to Malcom and exited the bleacher's with a large grin on her face knowing that she'd get to meet the handsome man one more time.

Chapter 2

Malcom was infatuated with Jane. Since last night, the beautiful redhead had been on his mind. As he strolled down Peachtree Avenue, he had a dozen looks from concerned white people. He was in the white part of town, but he didn't let the looks deter him. He was always used to being a fish out of water around white people.

As he neared Jane's home, he heard a police siren, and turned to find a police car riding up to him. A window was rolled down, and the white cop glared at Malcom.

"You lost boy?" He snarled.

"No, sir. I was invited to a classmate's house to study. The teacher assigned us a project." Malcom lied, showing him the books he had in his hands.

The cop stared at the books and chuckled. "Not only do they let you people in, now they are forcing ya'll to work together on projects? Shit, this country truly has gone to hell."

Malcom didn't say anything as he stared into the cops eyes. The two held a staring contest until the Cop spat tobacco towards Malcom. His spit landed near Malcom's shoes and the cop pointed towards Malcom. "Make sure you're out of here by sundown. You *don't* want to find out what happens if I catch you after that? You understand me, boy?"

"Yes, sir."

The cop nodded and then drove away.

Malcom watched the car drive down the street and took a sigh of relief. He wish that was the first time he was harassed by the cops, but as a black man in America, he was used to being constantly harassed by the police. He walked towards Jane's house and knocked on the door.

Jane answered the door and smiled at him.

"Malcom!"

"Hi Jane. I love your dress." He replied, admiring her pink outfit.

"Thank you. You look handsome as well. I like your blue shirt. Come on in."

Malcom followed Jane inside and she led him towards the living room, where the radio was located. Malcom looked around the room and watched as Jane walked towards the large brown stereo and fiddled with the dials. She turned it on and an upbeat Motown song was playing.

"Is this suitable for dancing?"

"Yes, it's perfect. I have a set list of moves that we could dance to."

"Wonderful."

"Let's start with the twist. The move I showed you last night."

"Oh, I've been practicing that one. Watch." Jane shimmied her hips and Malcom grinned.

"Perfect, can you do the mash potato?"

"Oh, I believe I know that one." Jane began moving her arms and legs.

"Yes, very good. Who says you needed a teacher. You're a natural at that move."

"Thank you."

Malcom began to dance with her. The two got closer, as they danced side by side. Malcom grabbed her hand and spun her around. Jane laughed as she twisted around into his arms. The two held each other close as they swing danced in the living room. Malcom picked her up and swung her around. Jane giggled as Malcom twisted and turned her around in various ways. By the time the song ended, the two held each other in close embrace staring to each others eyes, breathing deeply.

As Malcom looked at her, he felt that feeling he felt from the bleachers again. It made his heart flutter, and as he stared at her all he wanted to do was kiss her. Standing there, it was torture, not expressing his true feelings. He knew right there, he had to let her know how he felt.

"Jane?"

"Yes?"

"Dancing with you, has been amazing. However, I can't help but to feel there's something growing between us."

"I feel it too. An attraction maybe? I know my mind is telling me no, but my heart is..."

"Your heart is telling you yes?"

She nodded.

"I feel the same way. The world tells us that we shouldn't be together, yet wanting to be with you is the only thing I want."

"I want the same."

"However, we both know that whatever we want, ain't going to happen. A love between a black man and white woman, can't happen."

"Why not. We are both humans. Can't another human love another?"

Malcom shook his head. "America doesn't see me that way. In their eyes, we are still inferior slaves."

"I don't see you that way. I only see you as a handsome man."

"And I only see you as a beautiful woman."

"Then let us pursue what grows between us."

"Are you sure?"

"I've never been surer about something in my life."

Malcom reached out and touched Jane's chin. He felt her body tremble from his touch. The two locked eyes and Malcom inched closer to her. His lips hovered over her's, only a centimeter apart.

"I only want this if you want this." He whispered.

"I want this," she reassured.

Leaning forward, he placed his lips upon hers and his heartbeat tripled it's pace. Her lips felt smoother than silk as they slid across hers. His legs locked and his arms wrapped around Jane's as he held her close.

After their kiss, Jane pulled away from his lips and Malcom felt naked without her touch. He rubbed her cheek with his thumb and smiled.

"I liked that kiss." She grinned.

"As did I. I feel like a weight had been lifted off my shoulders."

"Mine too." She added. "Did you want to keep dancing?"

"I'd love too."

Malcom and Jane continued to dance through the afternoon, until Jane looked at the clock and cursed.

"Damn, my brother will be returning from practice soon."

"Oh, when I can I see you next?"

"Thursday. He has a late practice. We can dance again."

"I'd like that. I'll see you soon."

"See you soon."

The couple smiled at each other and Malcom leaned forward for another kiss. This second kiss was just as good as the first. After their embrace, Malcom held Jane and smiled before leaving the house.

As he walked down the street, his mind replayed the kiss that Jane and him shared, realizing that he had something special with Jane. He knew that being with Jane could bring trouble, but he didn't care about the cost. He only wanted her.

Chapter 3

Jane couldn't sleep as she laid in her bed. In her mind, she could only think of Malcom and the kiss that they shared. She couldn't explain why he was stuck in her brain. As she laid there, she heard a soft tap at her window and she jumped from her bed.

Looking at the window, she saw a shadowy figure, and she trembled as she asked, "is someone out there?"

"It's Malcom." The voice whispered.

"Malcom?" she exclaimed, getting out of bed. She opened her window and Malcom climbed into her bedroom. "Malcom, what are you doing here, you shouldn't be here! My brother is just in the other room. If he hears us…"

"I know, but I couldn't stop thinking of you. That kiss we shared earlier. I've never felt something like that before."

"Me either."

Malcom grinned. "I just wanted to come over and tell you what's in my heart. You've been on my mind all night and been driving me crazy."

"I'm mad about you too. I couldn't sleep because my mind is going crazy for you."

"Do you care if I stay the night? I want to be close to you."

"No, you can stay. Come, lay in bed with me."

The two laid down and Malcom wrapped his arm around Jane, cuddling close with her. Jane moved her body across his crotch attempting to get comfortable until she felt something stiff.

"Malcom?" she asked, turning in the bed to face him.

"I'm sorry Jane. Like you said, we're only human, and my basic urges have taken over. If you give me some space, I will control it."

Jane smiled and replied, "And what if I don't want you to control it? I have my own urges as well."

"Are you sure?" he asked.

Jane nodded. "I've wanted you since the first time we touched."

"As did I," Malcom replied. He stared into her eyes before passionately kissing her. As the two kissed, Malcom removed his shirt and pants to become naked. Jane, pushed the straps of her nightgown away, revealing her nude body to him.

Malcom grabbed her breast and massaged it, gently stroking the nipple with his thumb. Jane moaned from his hands touching her. Their lips once more met as they kissed. Slowly his hand sunk towards her wet center and she felt his finger enter inside. Her back arched as he touched her.

He soon shifted and stroked his stiffness. Jane's eyes opened wide as she stared at him.

"Are you sure I can have you?" He whispered.

"I am yours as you are mine." She replied.

Malcolm smiled and held her chin kissing her with such passion that he made her head spin. As they kissed, she felt him enter her.

She closed her eyes as a warm feeling spread throughout her body, and a soft moan left her lips. She had felt nothing like this before, she never felt more connected to a man than she did at that moment.

Feeling his body slide against hers, she held him tight. She didn't want to let go. She didn't want the pleasure to end. This man that she barely knew had managed to capture her heart. She was struck by Cupid's arrow and within two days, she'd fallen for this man. She couldn't explain why or how. There were a lot of factors that drove her. It could have been his kindness, his charm, or his body. She wasn't sure, but what she was sure about was this man felt amazing.

Every inch of him pulsed in between her legs and when it was all over she laid in the bed gasping for air as she was satisfied in every shape of the of the word.

As the young couple laid in bed, sweaty and exhausted, they stared into each other eyes. Not a word was shared as their actions proved what was in their hearts. Malcolm touched her cheek and smiled.

"That was amazing," he grinned.

"I enjoyed it as well."

"Did you want me to leave?" He asked.

Jane shook her head. "Can you stay with me the night?"

"I'd love too." Malcom kissed Jane and dragged her closer to him. The two cuddled in bed falling asleep with a newfound love.

Chapter 4

Jane woke up with the sun on her face. Looking toward her left, she saw a naked Malcom with his arm draped over her breast. She smiled looking at his face as he slept. She noticed his small button nose and realized how cute he was.

As she studied him, she heard her brother call out her name.

"Jane! Jane! Are you up?" He asked.

"Shit! Malcom wake up. My brother! He's coming over here!"

Malcom's eyes open wide as he jumped out of bed. "Shit, where are my clothes?"

"There's no time. Hide in my closet."

By the time Malcom got into her closet, the door opened up.

"Jane?"

"Fred!" Jane shrieked as she attempted to cover herself up.

"Oh, sorry," he replied covering his face.

Jane quickly grabbed her nightgown and placed it on.

"Why are you in here?" She growled.

" I heard noises in here, Jane. Was someone in here?"

"No, not at all it's just me."

Fred looked at his sister and snorted. "Bullshit. You were naked. You never sleep in the nude. You had a man over here."

"Okay, busted I did. Can you leave now?"

He smirked. "Well, well, my little sister is finally experiencing a college fling." Fred looked around the room and his cocky smile grew even larger. "Wait...is he still here?"

"No..."

His goofy grin was unbearable to Jane, as she wanted to wipe his smile off his face. Fred walked around the room, studying it's every detail. He picked up Malcom's clothes and held it in front of Jane. "He's still here, isn't he?"

"Yes, can you leave now? I promise it won't happen again." Jane reached for the clothes, but Fred held them high in the air, away from her grasp.

"Why are you pushing me out? I deserve to see this man who stole my sister's heart, an impossible feat, that I might add," he mocked. "Come out. Come out where ever you are!" Fred moved around the room. He checked under the bed and then walked towards the closet.

"Is he in here?" Fred asked.

"Please Fred..." Jane begged. Her heart moved rapidly as she knew it would be the end if he caught Malcom. She prayed that her brother would come to his senses and just leave the room like she asked.

Her brother ignored her pleas as he opened the closet. His smile disappeared as soon as he saw Malcom.

"A black man!" He shouted. "You raped her!" He accused.

"Wait!" Malcolm said as he placed his arms up in defense. However, Fred did not wait as his hands squeezed Malcolm's neck. Malcom gasped for air, attempting to fight back, but Fred was much stronger.

"Fred stop it! You're hurting him. He did no such thing!"

"This black man has tainted you! He raped you. Not a jury in this country would convict me for killing him."

"Fred stop it! He did not rape me. I wanted him. Stop!" Jane got out of bed and attempted to pull her brother off of him, but he shoved her off.

"Stop it Jane. Leave me be. Let me deal with this *savage*, and then you'll get yours."

"Fred! Stop!" Jane begged with tears rolling down her cheeks, but she realized that her brother wasn't going to stop. She saw the evil in his eyes, and she saw the life draining from Malcom's. She made a spilt decision and quickly picked up a nearby lamp. She smashed the ceramic vase on his head and Fred fell down letting go of Malcom.

Malcom fell to the ground and gasped for air.

"Oh, no. Did I kill him?" Jane asked.

Malcom checked his pulse and shook his head. "He still has a pulse."

"Oh, thank God. Are you okay?"

"Yes. Thank you for saving my life."

"I'd do anything for you. I couldn't explain this feeling that I had before, but now I know. I know what my heart is telling me, and what it is telling me is that I love you." Jane admitted.

I love you too." Malcom replied. "Like you, I can feel this feeling. It's a feeling of longing and now that I know you want the same, I can't help but to smile.

"What now?" Jane asked, looking at her brother.

"Runaway with me."

"You can't be serious?"

"I am. You love me and I love you. When your brother comes too he will be angry. It's best to leave now."

"Where will we go?"

"North. The northern states aren't as bad as the states down here. I know that we can start a new life there."

"I don't have much money..."

"I have enough to get us there. We'd get jobs, we'd get a house. Raise a family."

"You want a family with me?" Jane asked.

"Yes, I want to spend my life with you Jane. You are the only woman for me."

"And you are the only man. Wherever you, go I'll follow."

"Then follow me to a life where our love can be had. Follow me to a world where we can be together."

"Are you sure of it? What if the north is as bad as the south?"

"I'm not sure how the people will treat our love, but what I am sure of is love always wins. It is a greater force than hate, and in the end it will always prevail."

"Aww, Malcom. That was sweet. I want this more than ever. Let us leave this life and began anew. I love you, Malcom."

"And I love you Jane." Malcom held Jane's hands and stared into her eyes. Leaning forward he kissed her once more. After their embrace, the couple quickly gathered their things and ran out the door, to go and celebrate their newfound love and their new lives together.

Epilogue

"Jane are you in the kitchen?" Malcom asked walking into their small one bedroom house. "I have wonderful news."

"I am. I am feeding Tommy." She replied. Jane held out a spoonful of baby food attempting to feed their mixed child. Malcom walked into the kitchen and kissed his son and then Jane.

"What is the good news? She asked.

"I got promoted to shift manager at the factory."

"Really?"

Malcom nodded. "We did it. With the larger salary we can a afford a bigger house. No more will we struggle."

"That's great news. Oh Malcom, the last two years since we've ran away have been tough, but our marriage has never been stronger. Getting this promotion is all you ever wanted."

"It is, but in truth, what I care more about is providing for you and Tommy."

"Oh, Malcom." Jane smiled, hugging her husband.

As he held her he whispered, "You see, what did I tell you? Love always wins. I love you both."

"I love you too," Jane smiled before kissing her husband. As they kissed Jane grinned knowing that their bond was stronger than ever. It didn't falter when her brother threatened Malcom's life nor did it falter now. She couldn't be more happier in her life, and she thanks God for bringing Malcom to her when she needed him the most.

Don't miss out!

Visit the website below and you can sign up to receive emails whenever Remy Marie publishes a new book. There's no charge and no obligation.

https://books2read.com/r/B-A-HZLI-ACZMC

BOOKS 2 READ

Connecting independent readers to independent writers.

Also by Remy Marie

Short & Sweet Interracial Romance
Short & Sweet Interracial Romance: Bundle # 1
Finding True Love
My True Love
Always There
The First Date
Runaway With Me

Standalone
The Prince's Bride

Watch for more at https://remymarieromance.blogspot.com/?m=1.

About the Author

Remy Marie is a romance author who loves to write about charming heroes and brave heroines. While writing never came naturally for Remy, he continued to strengthen his craft, by constantly reading and writing. If he is not writing or reading, he is usually watching TV with his supportive wife, aggressively cheering for his college and professional sports teams, playing video games, or crunching numbers at his daytime job.

Read more at https://remymarieromance.blogspot.com/?m=1.

www.ingramcontent.com/pod-product-compliance
Lightning Source LLC
Chambersburg PA
CBHW022056150726
47990CB00003B/1117